Sam and the Gnome's Red Hat

Written and illustrated by
Admar Kwant

Floris
Books

Sam lived at the edge of a forest. Whenever he stepped outside, his friend robin flew up to say hello and sing for him.

Sam would tear up a piece of bread he'd saved for her. She would peck at the scattered crumbs and tilt her head to give him a cheerful look.

Sam's friend fawn was very shy,
but Sam understood. When fawn
was nowhere to be seen, Sam
would follow his tracks, staying
especially quiet and calm.

Sometimes fawn sprang
about gracefully for Sam,
and his forest-brown eyes
gave Sam a warm glance.

Sam's best friend lived in the middle of the forest where the ferns and mosses grew. Sam loved dropping by.

If his best friend wasn't home, Sam left something special: a sweet blackberry, a shiny pebble or a red woodpecker feather.

Sometimes when Sam had been out, he'd find something special left on his windowsill: a golden birch leaf with an insect-trail 'S' for Sam, or a snail's shell with bright coloured rings. He kept them in a cardboard box.

One night, Sam heard the voice of the wind change. Its usual softness turned into an angry bellow that rattled the roof. The door thudded, but Sam knew the wind couldn't get through. He was safe and warm inside.

He thought of robin, fawn and his best friend, out in the forest. Were they safe from the storm?

Next morning, the wind was back to soft fluttering and whispering.

As Sam walked into the forest, robin and fawn came to greet him.

Robin chirped and bobbed. "I'm so pleased you are cheerful after all that ruffling wind," said Sam.

Fawn stepped forward. "I'm glad the storm hasn't made you nervous," said Sam.

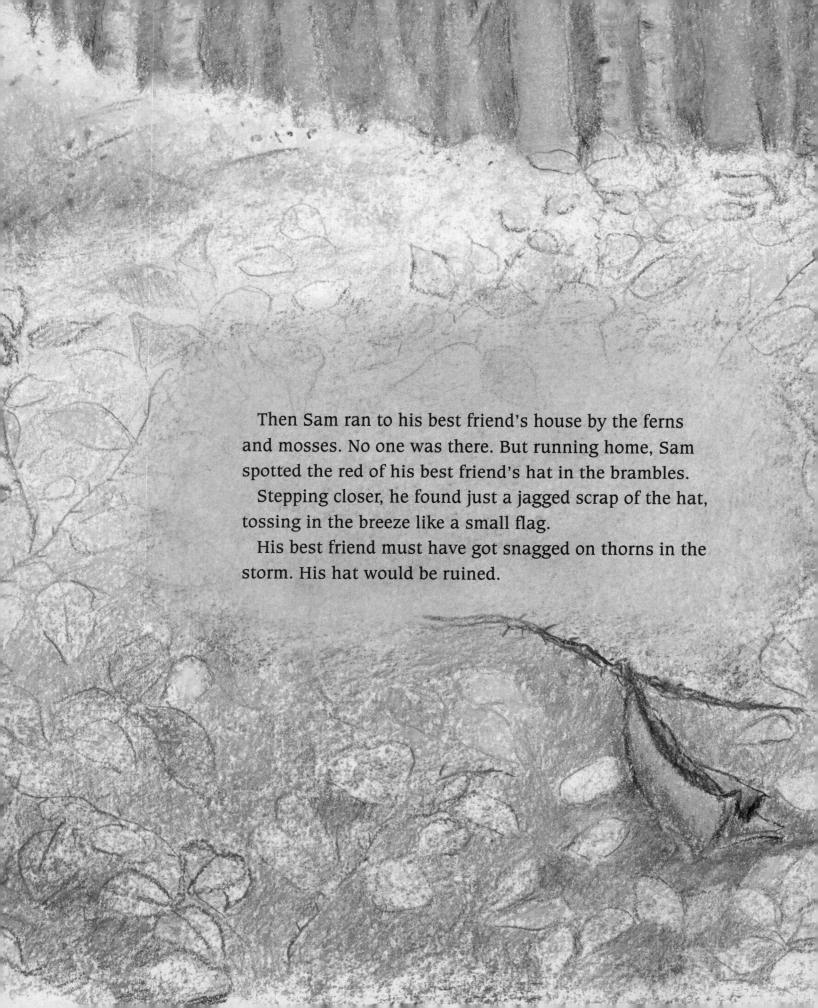

Then Sam ran to his best friend's house by the ferns and mosses. No one was there. But running home, Sam spotted the red of his best friend's hat in the brambles.

Stepping closer, he found just a jagged scrap of the hat, tossing in the breeze like a small flag.

His best friend must have got snagged on thorns in the storm. His hat would be ruined.

Granny had a basket of cloth pieces. Blue, green, yellow and red.
Soft and rough. Wool, cotton and silk, velvet and satin.
Sam found the warmest, softest piece, and rubbed it on his cheek.
Just right. He cut a hat shape and threaded the needle. Squeezing his
lips together, stitch by stitch, Sam sewed a
new hat for his best friend.

Finally, the hat was ready. Sam wrapped it in tissue paper and tied the parcel with a ribbon. Proudly, he skipped to the little house deep in the forest and left his gift on the mossy doorstep.

That night the cold sky was full of twinkling stars.
A warm-hearted gnome walked through the forest
to *his* best friend's house. He pulled his new red hat
snug over his ears.

Sam slept soundly. He didn't stir when
his best friend looked fondly at the quiet
house, nor when his best friend left a
new gift on the windowsill.

But he smiled in his sleep.

Sam found his gift the next morning.
It was a beautiful box for keeping his
treasures in, lined with soft red cloth
from an old hat.

He knew it was made with love.